TONY BRADMAN

DiLLY

THE ANGEL

Illustrated by Susan Hellard

MAMMOTH

First published in Great Britain 1990
Published 1991 by Mammoth
an imprint of Reed International Books Limited
Michelin House, 81 Fulham Road, London SW3 6RB
and Auckland, Melbourne, Singapore and Toronto

Reprinted 1993, 1994 (twice), 1995

Text copyright © 1990 Tony Bradman
Illustrations copyright © 1990 Susan Hellard

ISBN 0 7497 0432 2

A CIP catalogue record for this title
is available from the British Library

Printed and bound in Great Britain
by Cox & Wyman Ltd, Reading, Berkshire

Contents

DILLY AND THE BURGLAR

"Can we go home now?" said Dilly, tugging at Mother's sleeve. "I don't want to miss *The Deadly Dinobots*."

Mother, Dilly and I were standing in the hall of Mrs Dolf's house. She's Dilly's minder, which means she looks after him when Mother is at work.

The Deadly Dinobots is Dilly's favourite TV programme, so he was desperate to get home and watch it. Mother wasn't. She was too interested in what Mrs Dolf was telling her.

"What, Dilly?" she said. "Stop pulling my coat like that . . . You don't say, Mrs Dolf. That's the third burglary this week!"

"Mother," said Dilly, "what's a . . . burger-lary? Is it something you get at MacDinosaurs?"

Mother and Mrs Dolf laughed.

"Don't you know anything, silly Dilly?" I said. "It's when someone gets into your house and steals all your best stuff."

Dilly didn't believe I was telling the truth, so Mother had to do some explaining.

She told him that bad dinosaurs do sometimes break into other dinosaurs' houses to take their things. In fact, Mrs Dolf's neighbour, Mrs Daffa, had been burgled just last night.

"The family were upstairs asleep," said Mrs Dolf. "They didn't hear a thing . . . The Dino-police said the burglar must have got in through a window. Luckily not much was taken, just some money and the TV set. Mrs Daffa was pretty upset, though. She says she's going to get a burglar alarm."

Dilly asked what a burglar alarm was.

Mother explained it was something that made a loud noise when a burglar tried to open a window or a door. The noise was to scare the burglar off and wake up the dinosaurs in the house.

"Does it make a *very* loud noise?" Dilly asked.

"I don't really know, Dilly," said Mother. "Although I should think the louder it is, the better it works."

Dilly didn't say anything to that. But I could see he had his very thoughtful look on his face.

Mother and Mrs Dolf talked for a while longer, then Mother glanced at her watch.

"Goodness, look at the time!" she said.

We said goodbye to Mrs Dolf and her little dinosaur, Dilly's friend, Danni. Then Mother hurried us home. She had almost forgotten she was going out with Father that evening.

Our Aunt Dimpla was going to babysit. She was coming at seven o'clock, and there was a lot to do before then. So Mother asked us both to be well behaved and helpful.

But Dilly didn't want to be either.

At first he was just very sulky. Then he started throwing his toys around, and doing a lot of stamping, STAMP, STAMP, STAMP.

At dinner he wouldn't eat any toasted swamp worms, or even drink any of his pineapple juice.

"Whatever is wrong with you, Dilly?" said Father. "You're not usually like this when we go out, especially when Aunt Dimpla looks after you. I thought she was your favourite babysitter."

"She isn't," shouted Dilly. "I hate stupid old Dimpla . . . and I don't want you to go out."

Then he burst into tears.

Mother and Father looked at each other. They just didn't understand why Dilly was behaving this way. They can be very slow, sometimes.

"I know what's wrong with him," I said. "He's worried a burglar's going to get in while you're not here."

Dilly stuck his tongue out at me, but I was right, as we found out once he'd calmed down.

"I don't want a bad dinosaur to break into our house and steal our TV set, Father," he said. "I won't be able to watch *The Deadly Dinobots* then."

"Don't worry about it, Dilly," said Father. "No one's going to do that while Aunt Dimpla's here."

"But what if she falls asleep?" said Dilly. His bottom lip was trembling, and he looked as if he might start crying again. "A burglar might come up to my room and steal all my toys."

Father put his arm round Dilly's shoulders.

"Listen, Dilly," he said. "If you want, I'll tell Aunt Dimpla not to fall asleep, and I'll make sure the windows are locked before we go out. I promise we won't be late, and as soon as we get back I'll come up and check on you. Now is that OK?"

Dilly paused . . . then he said it was, although I could see he still didn't look very happy.

Just then Aunt Dimpla arrived, and Mother and Father had to go. They told Dilly not to worry, then kissed us both goodbye.

We watched TV for a while, then Aunt Dimpla said it was Dilly's bedtime. I thought he might make a fuss, but he didn't. He *did* make Aunt Dimpla look under his bed though, just to make sure a burglar wasn't hiding under it.

When it was my bedtime, Aunt Dimpla came upstairs with me. We both looked in on Dilly. He was lying flat on his back with his arms by his sides. His eyes were shut tight. Aunt Dimpla said he looked very sweet when he was asleep.

I didn't say anything.

I read for a while, then I felt sleepy. I was just about to doze off when I heard footsteps on the landing. I sat up and listened, my heart thudding

. . . all this talk of burglars had got *me* scared now. But then I thought it was probably only Aunt Dimpla going to the bathroom, so I went to sleep.

I was right in the middle of a wonderful dream about not having a little brother when a terrific noise woke me up – CRASH!

Straight after that there was another noise. And if you thought it might have been an ultra-special, 150-mile-per-hour super-scream, you'd be exactly right. What's more, it was the loudest one I'd ever heard.

I jumped out of bed and ran to Dilly's bedroom.

It was in a terrible mess. There were toys scattered everywhere, and bits of what looked like the potted fern plant Mother keeps in her bedroom. Only it wasn't potted any more. The pot was smashed, and there was soil all over the carpet.

There was something else on the carpet too, or rather, *someone*, I should say. It was a grown-up dinosaur who was just getting to his feet.

Dilly stopped screaming when I came into his room.

"Look out, Dorla!" he shouted. "It's the burglar!"

Of course, it wasn't a burglar. It was Father, who had come up to check on Dilly as he'd promised he would. But it took us ages to quieten Dilly down and make him realise that.

It turned out Dilly had only pretended to be asleep earlier. As soon as he knew I'd gone to bed and Aunt Dimpla wouldn't come upstairs any more, he'd started building his own burglar alarm, a very simple one.

He'd just made a huge pile of things behind his door. He'd used toys, the chair that goes with his little desk, his lamp, and even some things from Mother and Father's bedroom — including the potted fern plant. That explained the footsteps on the landing.

The idea was that a burglar would trip over the pile, and the noise would wake Dilly up. Then he would scream to frighten the burglar off, and wake everyone else up at the same time.

Father had a big bruise on his leg, and I could tell he was a little cross. Mother behaved as if she were cross, too, but I'm sure I heard her giggle once or twice, especially when Father started to limp.

She did tell Dilly off about the plant, though. He said he was sorry, and that he'd only been trying to help keep us safe from burglars.

The next day, Father told Dilly he'd been thinking about getting a proper burglar alarm fitted anyway.

"But will you be able to get one as loud as my scream, Father?" said Dilly, with a serious look on his face.

Father smiled.

"I shouldn't think so, Dilly," he said. "I can't imagine they make one *that* loud."

DILLY AT THE FUNFAIR

"Is it *today* we're going to the funfair, Father?" asked Dilly at breakfast.

Father sighed. He doesn't like funfairs, and I could tell he wasn't looking forward to our outing.

"Yes, Dilly," he said. "We'll leave straight after breakfast."

"What's wrong, dear?" Mother asked with a smile. She *loves* funfairs, and can't understand why Father doesn't. She'd been teasing him ever since we'd decided to go. "I'm sure you'll have a *wonderful* time. We all will, won't we, Dilly?"

Dilly nodded, and ran out of the kitchen. A few seconds later we heard him calling from the hall.

"I'm ready! I'm ready!" he was shouting.

He was standing by the front door with his coat on inside out, and his shoes on the wrong feet. He was so excited he just couldn't keep still.

Not long after, we set off in the dino-car. Dilly didn't stop talking all the way. Mother had already told him about the funfair, but he wanted her to tell him again. So she described the rides, and the booths where you can win prizes.

"I'm going to win a prize!" he said. "I just know I will!"

After that, he must have asked Mother and Father at least 100 times if we had arrived yet. Then we saw the first sign leading to the funfair, and Mother read it out.

"Motorway Exit Three for Dino-World," she said. "A Feast Of Fun For All The Family . . . "

"Hurray!" cheered Dilly.

He went quiet when we got to the gate. Beyond the fence you could see some of the rides. There was a huge roller coaster, a Big Wheel, and lots of other amazing things. Dilly just stared with his mouth open.

The car-park was practically full, but we found a space in the end. Dilly started running in the direction of the rides as soon as he got out of the dino-car. Father had to chase him, and Mother said he wasn't to run off.

"We don't want you getting lost, Dilly, do we?" she said.

I wouldn't have minded losing him for a while, but I didn't say anything.

At last we were inside. There were so many fantastic rides we didn't know which one to try first.

"Can we go on that, Father?" said Dilly. Father didn't say anything. He just looked up and gulped.

Dilly was pointing at the huge roller coaster we'd seen from outside. We walked over to it, and saw it was called *The Tyrannosaurus Run*. It looked *really* scary.

There was a queue of dinosaurs waiting to go on it, and a dinosaur taking their money.

Dilly wanted to get on it straightaway. But the dinosaur who was taking the money said he was too young. I wasn't, though, and that made Dilly very cross.

"It's not fair!" he said, and stamped his foot.

Mother explained that the ride was probably a little *too* scary for a dinosaur of his age.

"You can come on The Big Wheel with me instead," she said with a smile, "while Father takes Dorla on *The Tyrannosaurus Run*. I'm sure he just can't wait."

Father didn't look so sure, but he didn't get a chance to say anything. Dilly grabbed Mother's paw and dragged her off.

The Tyrannosaurus Run was even more amazing than I thought it was going to be. The scariest part was when it twisted over straight after a loop-the-loop.

When we got off, I told Father I'd really enjoyed it, and asked him if he had, too. He said he had, but I'm not sure if he was telling the truth. He looked a little pale green.

We went to find the others. I was expecting to see Dilly and Mother high in the air, but they weren't on The Big Wheel at all. They were on the ground, and Dilly was looking fed up.

"Never mind, Dilly," Mother was saying. "Being scared isn't anything to be ashamed of."

Father asked what was wrong. It turned out that Dilly hadn't liked The Big Wheel at all. He'd been OK at the beginning, but when they'd got to the top he'd told Mother he wanted to get off. She had to ask the dinosaur in charge if he would stop The Big Wheel in the middle of the ride.

Dilly soon cheered up when Father asked if he'd like some sugared swamp floss. It comes on a stick, and it's made from lots of thin strands of swamp fern covered in crushed sugar cane. Dilly and I both love it.

But that was the last thing Dilly enjoyed. I'm sorry to say he didn't have a very good time at Dino-World. He wasn't allowed to go on a lot of the rides because he was too young. And when he *was* allowed, he was usually too frightened.

Mother thought he'd like the Dactyl Bombers, for instance. But they made too much noise when they dived, and we had to ask if he could get off early. I thought they were terrific, and went on three times in a row with Father. I'm not sure if he enjoyed them, though. He went pale green again.

When we'd been on all the rides, we tried out some of the booths. In one you had to throw hoops over bowls with swamp lizards in. In another, you

had to knock over piles of fern cones
with rocks. Dilly kept saying he was
sure to win a prize.

He didn't. For a start, he was too
small to see over the side of some of
the booths. And even when Father
picked him up so he could throw the
hoops or the rocks, he kept missing.

I didn't miss, though. I won a cuddly Stegosaurus toy, a funny hat and a big bag of candied fern flakes. Dilly was *so* jealous.

"I hate you, smelly old Dorla!" he shouted at me, and stomped off, STOMP, STOMP, STOMP.

It was time to go, anyway. Mother said we'd spent all our money, so we started making our way back to the car-park. Father looked relieved.

Just near the gate, we saw something very interesting. It was a Test-Your-Strength machine. You had to hit the bottom of the machine with a big wooden hammer, then it told you how strong you were. If you hit it *really* hard, a bell rang and you got a prize.

We stopped and watched some dinosaurs trying their luck. One of them had great big muscles, and we all thought he'd make the bell ring. But he didn't get anywhere near it.

Mother laughed, and told Father he ought to have a go. Father said he would, but only if Dilly had a turn first. I think he was trying to cheer him up. But Dilly just scowled and stamped his foot.

"I don't want a turn!" he shouted. "I hate machines like that . . . and I *hate* Dino-World too!"

And then . . . that's right, you guessed it, he opened his mouth and let rip with an ultra-special, 150-mile-per-hour super-scream, the kind that makes bells on Test-Your-Strength-Machines ring, and ring, and ring.

It was still ringing when Dilly stopped screaming. The dinosaur running the machine said he'd never

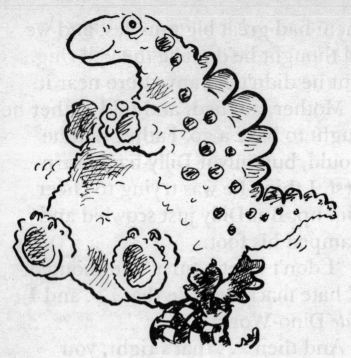

heard anything like it. He also said
Dilly could have any prize he wanted,
so long as he didn't come back ever
again.

Dilly was very pleased, and chose
the biggest cuddly Stegosaurus toy the
dinosaur had. It was *much* bigger than
mine.

On the way home in the dino-car, Dilly couldn't stop smiling.

"Can we come to the funfair again tomorrow, Mother?" he said at last.

"That would be nice, wouldn't it?" said Mother. She poked Father in the shoulder. "What do you say, Father?"

"Er . . . well . . . " Father started to say. Mother laughed.

"Maybe not *quite* so soon, Dilly," she said. "I don't think some of us are up to it!"

Father stuck his tongue out at Mother . . . and we all laughed!

DILLY DOES SOME MENDING

The other day, Father loaded the washing machine with dirty clothes and turned it on. But instead of making its usual noise, it just clunked and rattled.

"What's wrong with it, Father?" said Dilly.

He was sitting on the floor playing with his toy dino-cars. He's always been crazy about dino-cars, and everything to do with them.

"I don't know, Dilly," said Father, scratching his head. "I think we'll have to call someone out to mend it."

The repair dinosaur came that afternoon. She brought a big fern pod of tools with her and soon got to work. She clanked and banged for ages.

Dilly was fascinated. He hung around and got in the way, and asked lots of questions. But the repair dinosaur was very nice and didn't seem to mind.

Finally the washing machine was fixed, and the repair dinosaur went. But from that moment on, Dilly wouldn't stop talking about her.

"So would *you* like to be a repair dinosaur when you grow up, Dilly?" asked Mother with a smile.

"No, Mother," said Dilly. Mother looked surprised. "I want to be a repair dinosaur *now*. Can I mend something for you? *Please!*"

"You could try fixing some of your toys," said Mother. "An awful lot of them seem to be broken."

Dilly liked that idea. He asked Mother if he could have something to keep tools in like the repair dinosaur. She gave him an old fern pod and found a few things to put in it, like a little screwdriver and a plastic hammer from one of his old baby games. He was really pleased and ran off to his bedroom.

I went up to my bedroom, too. I wanted to listen to my new Rex and the Rockosaurs tape. But it started to sound very strange, so I went to ask Mother if she would have a look at my cassette player.

"OK, Dorla," she said. "I'd better come and see what Dilly's doing anyway. He's very quiet . . . which means he's probably up to no good!"

Mother was right, as she discovered when we went upstairs.

"Dilly!" she said. "What on earth have you done?"

Mother was standing in the doorway to Dilly's bedroom. I peeked round from behind her.

Dilly was sitting in front of his toy cupboard. He'd taken all the toys out of it and spread them everywhere.

"It took me most of yesterday morning to tidy those toys away," Mother said. "Now look at them. I thought you were going to mend some broken toys, not make a mess!"

"But I *am*, Mother. I'm mending this dino-car," said Dilly. "All its wheels are missing, and I can't find them *anywhere*."

"I'm not surprised," said Mother. "You won't find anything until you've tidied up, and you can start *now*. And don't stop the moment I'm gone – I'll be right next door in Dorla's room, making sure there's nothing wrong with her cassette player."

"But Mother . . . ".

"There are no 'buts' about it, Dilly," said Mother. "Just get your room tidied!"

Mother couldn't find anything wrong with my cassette player, so we decided it was probably the Rex and the Rockosaurs tape that was the problem. Then Mother had to go back downstairs to keep an eye on the swamp stew she was cooking.

Supper time soon came round. Father called us to the table, and when Dilly appeared, he had his I've-

Done-Something-That-Makes-Me-
Feel-Very-Clever look on his face.

"Have you tidied your room, Dilly?"
asked Mother as she put his plate in
front of him.

"Er . . . not quite, Mother," he said.
"I've been doing some mending
instead. I've been repairing Dorla's
cassette player."

"You've been doing *what*?" I yelled.

"I've been repairing your cassette
player, Dorla," he said. Then he
frowned. "But I can't seem to make it
work . . ."

I didn't want to hear any more. I
dashed upstairs.

My cassette player was lying on its
side with the back off and some wires
hanging out. I was so upset I burst
into tears.

It wasn't as bad as it looked, though.

Mother pushed the wires in and put the back on. She checked everything else and changed the batteries, and when I turned it on it sounded OK.

Mother gave Dilly a telling off, and then Father said he'd been silly, too. Young dinosaurs should never take the backs off electrical things, he said. They're very dangerous, and can give you a nasty shock.

Dilly did say he was sorry. But being told off certainly didn't stop him wanting to be a repair dinosaur. If anything, he got even worse over the next few days.

One evening, Mother found him trying to take the dino-phone to pieces. He'd actually undone a couple of the little screws. And the very next day, Father found him banging on the pipes under the sink with his plastic hammer. He refused to stop, and Father had to drag him out by his tail.

After that, Dilly was banned from touching *anything* he might damage. He kept asking if he could mend something, but Mother and Father wouldn't let him. He didn't like it. I could see him getting more and more cross every time they said no.

A few days later it was Saturday. Mother said we had to go to The Shopping Cavern, so after breakfast we all went out to the dino-car. We got in, and Father turned the ignition key. The engine didn't start.

"Oh no," said Father. "That's all we need."

Father got out and before anyone could stop him, Dilly climbed into the driving seat.

"Wow!" said Dilly. He moved the steering wheel from side to side and started pressing all the buttons. "This is great . . . broom, beep, beep!"

"Don't do that, Dilly," said Father. He opened the front of the dino-car to look at the engine. As soon as Dilly saw that, he jumped out. Mother got into the driver's seat.

"Can I help you mend it, Father?"

said Dilly. "There's nothing I'd rather fix than a *real* dino-car. Can I? *Please*?"

"I don't think so, Dilly," said Father. "And try not to get in the way. Umm . . . I can't see anything wrong. Try the engine again, dear."

Mother tried, but the engine wouldn't start.

"Father," said Dilly quietly. "I *love* dino-cars, and I *want* to help you mend it."

He had a look about him I'd seen before.

"The answer's still no, Dilly," said Father. He was about to say something else to Mother, but he didn't get the chance.

Dilly looked at him, opened his mouth . . . and let rip with an ultra-special, 150-mile-per-hour super-scream that went on, and on, and on.

And when he stopped screaming at
last, he gave one of the dino-car's
wheels a terrific kick.

Of course, Father was very cross.
He told Dilly off and said he had to go
indoors. It looked as if the dino-car
wasn't going to start, and Father said
he didn't want Dilly hanging around if
we had to call someone out to fix it.

"Maybe I'll give it one more try,"
said Mother. She turned the ignition
key . . . and the engine started!

"I mended it! I mended it!" shouted Dilly from the bedroom window, and nothing Mother or Father said could convince him he hadn't.

At The Shopping Cavern, Dilly told Father not to worry if the dino-car broke down again. He said he knew all about dino-cars, and that he was the best repair dinosaur in the whole world. If it did, he would just scream and give the wheel another kick.

Father gave Dilly a hard look. For a second I thought he was going to say something, but he didn't. He just shook his head instead.

DILLY AND THE CHRISTMAS PLAY

When Dilly came out of nursery
school the other day, he had a letter to
give to Mother. He looked worried
about it, too.

"What's the letter about, Mother?"
he asked. "Does it say I've been
naughty?"

"No, Dilly," said Mother with a
smile. "It says you're going to be
putting on a play for Christmas."

Dilly asked her what that meant.

Mother said a play was a way of telling a story. You had to dress up and pretend to be other dinosaurs. You would have words to say, and songs to sing. Dilly's class would have to practise the play, and then they would act it out for the Mothers and Fathers.

"Now doesn't that sound exciting, Dilly?" said Mother. "Which part do you think you're going to get?"

"The main one of course," said Dilly. "I'm going to be the *star*."

I laughed, and said there wouldn't be any parts for naughty little dinosaurs who screamed a lot. Dilly got cross and called me a rude name.

"That will do, you two," said Mother. "We'll just have to wait and see what part you're given, Dilly."

We didn't have to wait very long. The very next day at home time, all the little dinosaurs from Dilly's class came out chattering about the play.

All of them, that is . . . except Dilly.

He was the last one to come out. He walked towards us very slowly, with his tail trailing along behind him. He looked very, very fed up.

"Whatever is the matter, Dilly?" said Mother.

Dilly didn't answer. He didn't say a word all the way home, and when we arrived, he just flopped down on the sofa.

Mother gave us a drink and some crispy fern cookies. They're Dilly's favourites, but he didn't even look at them.

"Come on, Dilly," said Mother at last. "Tell me what's wrong."

It turned out Dilly hadn't got the main part. His friends Dixie and

Darryl were going to be playing the most important characters.

"So what part *did* you get, Dilly?" asked Mother.

"I'M GOING TO BE . . . AN ANGEL!" shouted Dilly.

Father spluttered, and nearly choked on his swamp tea. Then he laughed so hard he had to leave the room. Mother laughed too, and said it made a change from Dilly being a little devil. But Dilly didn't think it was very funny. He stamped off to his bedroom and slammed the door.

We found out a little more about it the next day, when Mother talked to Mrs Dactyl. Everyone who didn't have a speaking part in the play was going to be an angel. They would sing most of the songs, and they would have the best costumes, too.

"So it's not really *that* bad, Dilly," said Mother."

"But I don't want to be the same as everyone else!" he said.

Mother said she thought he would get more excited about the play when they started practising it. She also thought he'd enjoy helping her with the costume. But he didn't want to.

She used an old white sheet, and decorated it with lots of gold buttons and silver thread. She also bought some silver tinsel, the kind you put on

the Christmas tree. The idea was for Dilly to wear it round his head like a halo.

"There you are, Dilly," said Mother. She made him try it on. "You'll be the best-looking angel in the whole play!"

"No I won't," said Dilly, but he seemed quite impressed by the costume.

Mother was beginning to get a little worried. If there's one thing you can say about Dilly, it's that he's very stubborn. Once he decides he doesn't want to do something, it's very hard to get him to change his mind.

Mother and Father talked about it one evening. Then they asked me if I would try to get him interested.

I've been in lots of school plays, and I've played all sorts of parts. I was even an angel once myself. I was the *chief* angel, though, as I told Dilly when I went up to his room to talk to him.

"But I do know how you must feel, Dilly," I said. He didn't say anything. "It *is* nice to have the main part. I was just as upset as you are when we did *Dinorella* last year and I didn't get to be the star. I was only one of the other dinosaurs at the ball. A very important dinosaur, mind you, but it's not the same . . ."

"You should have been one of the

ugly sisters," said Dilly, and stuck his tongue out at me.

"At least they didn't have a horrible little brother," I said, and stuck my tongue out at *him*.

But Dilly's mood *did* begin to improve as the big day got closer. Gradually Dilly started to talk about the play. I could tell he was beginning to get excited.

Then one day after school, he was *bursting* to tell us some news.

"Guess what, Mother!" he said. "I've got some words to say!"

It turned out Mrs Dactyl had decided somebody needed to introduce the play, and Dilly had been given the job.

He had his words written down on a small card, and from then on that was all we heard. He practised them

48

morning, noon and night, until we all knew them as well as he did.

The day of the play arrived at last, and Dilly couldn't wait to get to school. The performance was going to be in the morning, so he had to get changed into his costume at home.

I have to say he looked pretty good, although he did look a little odd when he put his ordinary coat on – from behind, you could see part of the costume hanging down.

But when we got to Dilly's school, we found that everything was in

chaos. All the little dinosaurs were so
excited, and Mrs Dactyl couldn't seem
to control them. The Mothers and
Fathers were making lots of noise, too.

"Angels on stage now, please,"
shouted Mrs Dactyl.

Dilly and all the other little
dinosaurs who were dressed as angels
lined up on the stage. Dilly came
forward and stood right in the centre.
The dinosaurs behind him were very
excited, and couldn't stop chattering.

The audience didn't seem to have
noticed him either. The Mothers and
Fathers were too busy finding their
seats and saying hello to each other.
There were baby dinosaurs crying,
and teachers calling out.

Dilly started saying his words, but
no one was listening. He stopped,
tried again, but still no one listened.
He looked quite cross. I had a feeling
I knew what he was going to do next.

He opened his mouth, and let rip

with an ultra-special, 150-mile-per-hour super-scream, the kind that makes everyone go absolutely quiet and still *instantly*.

"Well, Dilly," said Mrs Dactyl in the silence after he stopped screaming. "I never thought I'd say this, but thank you for doing that. And now . . . on with the show!"

The play went very well. Dilly couldn't stop smiling all through it, and he sang as loud as he could. And of course, everyone talked about him afterwards, so in a way, he turned out to be the star after all.

On the way home, Mother said she hoped Dilly's performance meant he was going to be an angel all the time from now on.

Dilly said he would be. But I don't think he will . . . do you?

Tony Bradman

DILLY AND THE GHOST

After Dilly persuades Father to read him ghost stories at bedtime, he's positive the house is haunted. But no-one in the family believes him. So Dilly decides to convince everyone that there really are ghosts about the house . . .

This is the seventh collection of stories about Dilly, the world's naughtiest dinosaur.

Tony Bradman

DILLY GOES SWAMP WALLOWING

previously published as
Dilly the Worst Day Ever

In this fifth collection of stories about
Dilly, the world's naughtiest dinosaur,
Dilly causes mayhem at the library, goes
swamp wallowing and promises to be
good for a whole year — but I don't think
he can be, do you?

MEET THE WORLD'S NAUGHTIEST DINOSAUR

Even though, as everyone knows, he's the world's naughtiest dinosaur Dilly still has lots of fans. Now that he is so famous he's started making special visits to bookshops to meet the people who enjoy reading about him. You might be able to meet him in your local bookshop – he usually tries to behave himself!

You can write to this address for more information about Dilly and his books and about other books published by MAMMOTH.

MAMMOTH Press Office,
38 Hans Crescent,
London SW1X 0LZ

A Selected List of Fiction from Mammoth

While every effort is made to keep prices low, it is sometimes necessary to increase prices at short notice. Mandarin Paperbacks reserves the right to show new retail prices on covers which may differ from those previously advertised in the text or elsewhere.

The prices shown below were correct at the time of going to press.

☐	7497 1421 2	**Betsey Biggalow is Here!**	Malorie Blackman	£2.99
☐	7497 0366 0	**Dilly the Dinosaur**	Tony Bradman	£2.99
☐	7497 0137 4	**Flat Stanley**	Jeff Brown	£2.99
☐	7497 0983 9	**The Real Tilly Beany**	Annie Dalton	£2.99
☐	7497 0592 2	**The Peacock Garden**	Anita Desai	£2.99
☐	7497 0054 8	**My Naughty Little Sister**	Dorothy Edwards	£2.99
☐	7497 0723 2	**The Little Prince (colour ed.)**	A. Saint-Exupery	£3.99
☐	7497 0305 9	**Bill's New Frock**	Anne Fine	£2.99
☐	7497 1718 1	**My Grandmother's Stories**	Adèle Geras	£2.99
☐	7497 0041 6	**The Quiet Pirate**	Andrew Matthews	£2.99
☐	7497 1930 3	**The Jessame Stories**	Julia Jarman	£2.99
☐	7497 0420 9	**I Don't Want To!**	Bel Mooney	£2.99
☐	7497 1496 4	**Miss Bianca in the Orient**	Margery Sharp	£2.99
☐	7497 0048 3	**Friends and Brothers**	Dick King Smith	£2.99
☐	7497 0795 X	**Owl Who Was Afraid of the Dark**	Jill Tomlinson	£2.99
☐	7497 0915 4	**Little Red Fox Stories**	Alison Uttley	£2.99

All these books are available at your bookshop or newsagent, or can be ordered direct from the address below. Just tick the titles you want and fill in the form below.

Cash Sales Department, PO Box 5, Rushden, Northants NN10 6YX.
Fax: 01933 414047 : Phone: 01933 414000.

Please send cheque, payable to 'Reed Book Services Ltd.', or postal order for purchase price quoted and allow the following for postage and packing:

£1.00 for the first book, 50p for the second; **FREE POSTAGE AND PACKING FOR THREE BOOKS OR MORE PER ORDER.**

NAME (Block letters) ....

ADDRESS ....

....

☐ I enclose my remittance for ....

☐ I wish to pay by Access/Visa Card Number

Expiry Date

Signature ....

Please quote our reference: MAND